Rosie With Rose-Colored Glasses

By Jane Larson Wipf

Illustrations By Susan Raasch

In the teamship to launch *Rosie* I give thanks for the presence of:

God
My husband, Mike
Clayton, Hope, Tyler and Kristin Jackson
Maren Wipf, Ricardo Chamorro
Doris and Roland Larson
Michelle Stimpson

Susan Raasch, Laurie Ramirez, Tom Larson †, Jessica Raasch
Janet Griffing, Sarah Mallett, Mary Lee Larson, Bill Stimpson
Benito Ramirez, Brenda, Sarah and Paul Lamphere
Tommy †

Thanks also to those of you who have prayed, been enthused and believed!

Back cover photography: Jessica Raasch
Design and production: Laurie Ramirez
Printed by Litho Tech

Manufactured in the United States of America
ISBN: 978-0-9638512-1-5

Library of Congress Number: 2007904204

To order visit: www.sailingonhope.com

Or by mail, send $15.00 check or money order to:
3312 Decatur Lane
St. Louis Park, MN 55426

For Clayton and Hope
Hugs! ♡ Grandma Jane

To David, Naomi and Jessica
for your encouragement, patience and love.
"MaMa Sue"

Can you find the rose  in each picture?

"The light shines

in the darkness,

and the darkness

did not overcome it."

John 1:5

This is the tale of Rosie Rumbles:

An unusual light flooded the delivery room. "It's a girl!"

Rosie Rumbles came into the world one morning
at the crack of dawn. She was not a typical baby.
Rosie was born with rose-colored glasses!

Glittering in the sunlight streaming through the window,
the large frames graced Rosie's nose.

"Oh my!" exclaimed her mother.

"How odd," Rosie's father smiled thoughtfully.

They loved Rosie. Rosie loved life. And that was enough!

At bath time, Rosie's glasses steamed up.
She giggled as her mom taught her the alphabet,
drawing letters on the steamy glass.

Rosie was so bright-eyed there was
no need for a nightlight in her bedroom.

Rosie always slept on her back.
Can you guess why?

Rosie started skipping first, even before she learned to walk.

With the passing of years, Rosie fell in love with roses.
She smelled them everywhere she went.

Rosie loved life! ... and that was enough.

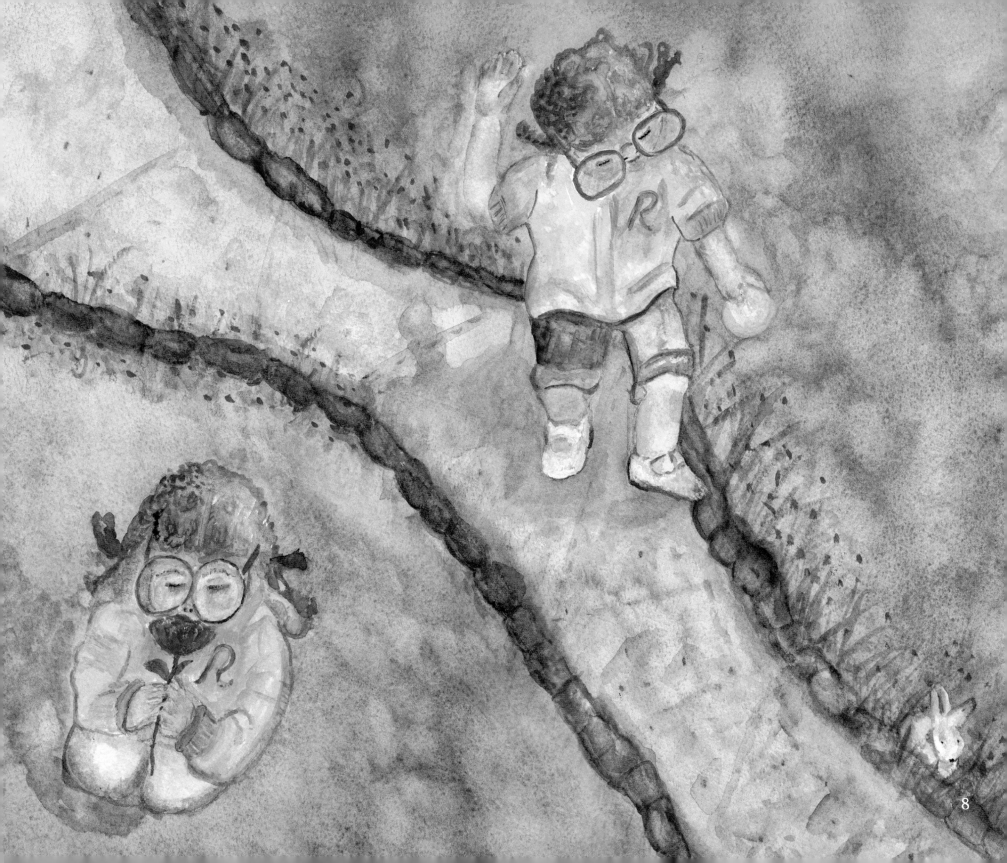

When Rosie saw a thunderstorm,
she would point at the crack of lightning in the sky
and see the silver lining
like she did
with so many things in life.

The rose-colored glasses were a part of Rosie.
Sometimes, Rosie's glasses slid down her nose in the heat
of the sun or when she was cooking her favorite breakfast,
which of course was eggs, sunnyside up.

Sometimes Rosie got teased about her rose-colored glasses.
Rosie didn't mind . . . most of the time.

Rosie loved people. Rosie would always see
the best in people. Rosie could see the light
in their hearts— even the people whose hearts
had grown dim or had closed.

Rosie saw what gifts and talents and strengths
people had— even before they knew!
Rosie encouraged them to do their best.

Rosie also loved animals and was nice to them.

Rosie had hope!

Rosie had more nicknames than most people.
Have you ever had a nickname?
They called Rosie: "Sliver of Light,"
"Sunshine," "Lady Upbeat," "Ms. Chin-Up,"
"Joy," and "Positive Plus."

Does it surprise you that the colors
that made her happiest were red and pink,
like the blush-colors that
came to her cheeks
when someone said
something very sweet to Rosie?

Do you have a favorite color?

One day Rosie almost lost her glasses.
She had been writing a story about looking on the bright side of life.
Rosie included a few Bible verses.

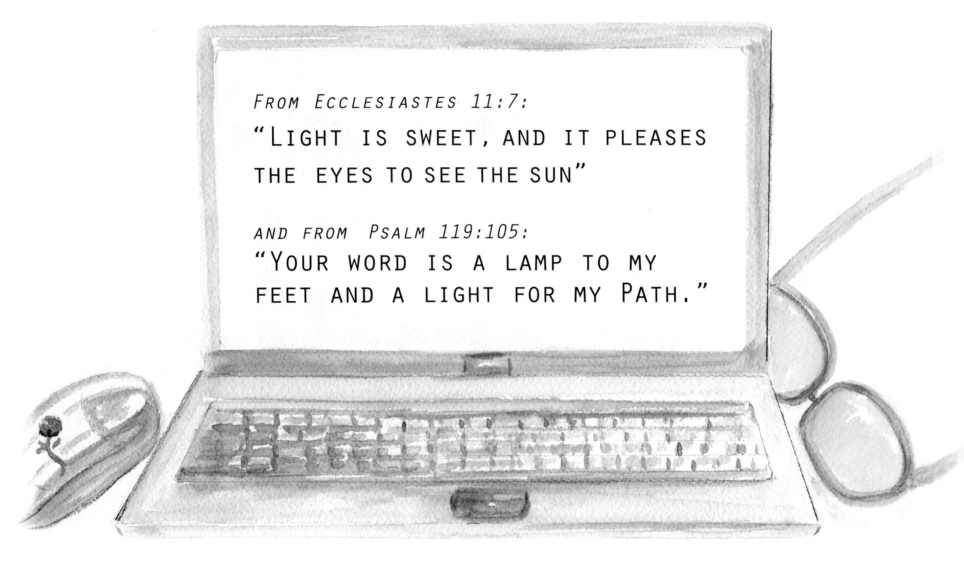

FROM ECCLESIASTES 11:7:
"LIGHT IS SWEET, AND IT PLEASES THE EYES TO SEE THE SUN"

AND FROM PSALM 119:105:
"YOUR WORD IS A LAMP TO MY FEET AND A LIGHT FOR MY PATH."

Rosie also talked about guarding your heart and being careful and kind with your words.

In the warm early September sun, a beautiful
purple and white butterfly landed on the notebook Rosie held
in her hands. This lovely creature struck her with awe.

As Rosie stretched her legs on the school lawn,
a young man named Stonewall Filibuster approached her.
So absorbed in the butterfly and the completion of
her writing project, Rosie was unaware of Stonewall.

As Stonewall Filibuster got closer, his dark shadow
fell across Rosie.

She looked up. His heavy boot
gave a swift kick to her precious work.

Rosie's papers and rose-colored glasses went flying.
The wings of the butterfly split in two.

In disgust, Filibuster laughed, "Dumb dreamer,
Rosie Rumbles. Who do you think you are? Get lost!"

Rosie Rumbles trembled with fear.
Her face turned red with anger. Rosie wanted
to say something to Stonewall but didn't.

As the bully stomped on Rosie's glasses,
he uttered a few more ugly words and then left.

Rosie's heart crumpled.

She felt like pins were sticking all over her.
Tears streamed down her face. Then, through blurry eyes,
Rosie saw her crushed glasses sparkling in the sun.

The rose-colored glasses were broken in many pieces…
but each piece laying in the grass caught the bright sunlight
just right so they created arched rainbows everywhere.

Rosie smiled.

As Stonewall walked away, Rosie raised her bare eyes toward his back. She saw that as he walked, the bottoms of his boots were enveloped in rainbows. Fragments of Rosie's rose-colored glasses had stuck to Stonewall. Rosie had touched him.

Puzzled, and with a compassionate sigh, Rosie looked down where she now kneeled. The butterfly whose wings had split in two was gone.

Rosie watched Stonewall Filibuster walk off in the distance. Suddenly, a purple and white butterfly landed on his right shoulder.

Joy filled Rosie's heart that day in a new way.

Years had come and gone when one day, Rosie ran into
Stonewall Filibuster at the very spot Rosie had last seen him.

He had changed. His face had softened. The chubby little hand
of a young girl eagerly hung onto Stonewall's left index finger.

"Rosie!" exclaimed Stonewall with delight, "It's been a long time."
"Yes," said Rosie. "It has been a very long time." "I'd like you to meet
my daughter," said Stonewall as he proudly looked upon the child.

As the little girl turned her face upwards into Rosie's, Rosie's face shone
with an unusual light. Stonewall's daughter had rose-colored glasses!
Looking into Rosie's eyes, Stonewall said, "I named her after you, Rosie."
Wiping away a tear, he said, "Her name is Rosie Joy."

Stonewall embraced Rosie with a warm hug. "I am so sorry
for how cruel I was, for how I treated you, beautiful Rosie Rumbles."

After a bit of silence, Rosie took a deep breath and said tenderly,
"I forgive you, Stonewall Filibuster."

In that moment, a purple and white butterfly circled the three and landed smack in the middle of Rosie Joy's rose-colored glasses.

She squealed with glee and said, "I know what! Let's get ice cream!"

Rain started pouring down, but you well know
it didn't matter because wherever Rosie with
rose-colored glasses went, there was bound to be sunshine.

"The light shines in the darkness,
and the darkness did not overcome it."

John 1:5

"In the world you will have trouble,

but be brave:

I have conquered the world."

– Jesus

John 16:33b

"Whatever is true, whatever is noble,

whatever is right, whatever is pure,

whatever is lovely, whatever is admirable—

if anything is excellent or praiseworthy—

think about such things.

Whatever you have learned or received or heard

from me, or seen in me—put it into practice.

And the God of peace will be with you ."

Philippians 4:8-9